# The Lonely Doll

*Story and Photographs*

## BY

## DARE

## WRIGHT

Houghton Mifflin Company
Boston

*To Edie,*

*who introduced me to Edith and the Bears*

Once there was a little doll. Her name was Edith. She lived in a nice house and had everything she needed except somebody to play with.

She was very lonely!

Every night when she said her prayers she pleaded,
"Please, please send me some friends."

Every morning when she ate breakfast all by herself
she sighed and wished for company.

Every day when she fed the pigeons she'd beg,
"Please stay and talk to me."
But the pigeons just ate and flew away.

Then one morning Edith looked into the garden and there stood two bears!

The big bear bowed. "You must be Edith," he said.
"I am Mr. Bear and this is Little Bear. We've come to be
your friends."

Edith clapped her hands with joy. "You must have
found me because I wished so hard," she cried.

Mr. Bear gave her head a kindly pat.

"Just wait and see what fun we'll have!" Little Bear whispered in Edith's ear.

She had never met any bears before, but she liked them at once.

From then on Edith was never lonely again.

Little Bear was right. They did have fun!

Of course Mr. Bear made Edith and Little Bear do
their lessons every day, but there was lots of time left
for adventures.

When they were good Mr. Bear took them to all
kinds of interesting places. They went to the park—

they went to the beach—

they went fishing!

But when they were naughty

Mr. Bear had to scold them

because they got too dirty—

or climbed

too high—

or went too far away alone.

One rainy day Mr. Bear left Edith and Little Bear
home by themselves.

"Now, don't you get into any trouble," he said.

"I hate rain," Edith grumbled crossly. "Why couldn't Mr. Bear take us with him? There's nothing for us to play indoors."

"We'll find something," said Little Bear. "Come on, let's explore the house."

They discovered a beautiful dressing room
with a big mirror.

Edith climbed up to look at herself and got very
cross indeed.

"My hair looks dreadful, and I'm tired of this old
dress," she muttered.

"Look what I've found," called Little Bear. "A whole closetful of clothes! Let's dress up."

"Oh, let's," agreed Edith, "but first I must do something about my hair."

She tried making it into a knot. That looked very
grown up.

"Try a flower," offered Little Bear.

He snatched a rose from a vase.

All the water spilled, but Edith didn't care.

Then came high-heeled shoes—

and a ruffled petticoat—

and a hat with roses and ribbons—

and Little Bear discovered the jewel box.

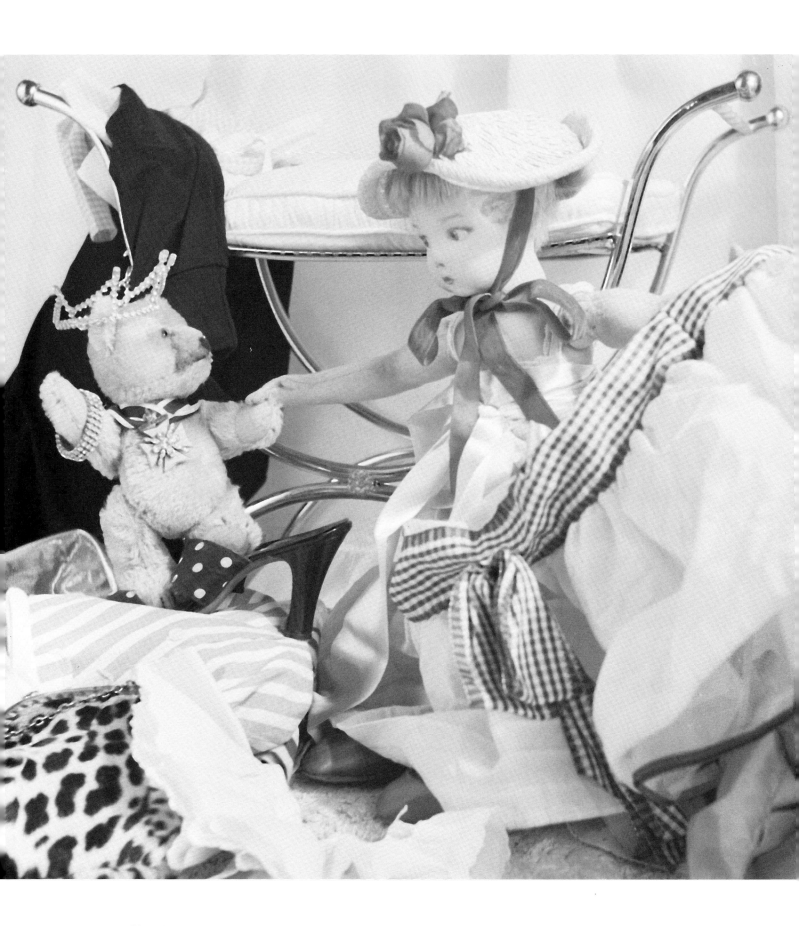

Finally they stopped to admire each other!

"All you need now, Edith, is lipstick," Little Bear said.

"Oh, I'd never dare," Edith worried. "You know what Mr. Bear would say."

"Who cares what Mr. Bear says? I don't!" cried Little Bear.

He grabbed the lipstick and scrawled all across
the mirror—
    "Mr. Bear is just a silly old thing!"

So on went the lipstick! But in the mirror Edith saw
Mr. Bear watching!

"Just look at this mess!" he said sternly. "These
things aren't yours. And you know you're too young for
lipstick, Edith."

"I am not!" replied Edith. "And I don't care what you say, anyway. You're a silly."

"I may be a silly," Mr. Bear answered, "but I know when a naughty little girl needs a spanking."

Little Bear couldn't watch. He was afraid his turn was next.

He was right!

"Now clean up every bit of this mess. And, Edith,
stop that crying!" Mr. Bear ordered sharply as he left.

But Edith went on crying as if her heart would break.

"Oh, stop it," grumbled Little Bear. "Isn't it just like a girl to cry because she gets spanked!"

"It's not that," Edith sobbed. "I'm scared."

"Scared?" Little Bear snorted. "Scared of what?"

"Mr. Bear's so angry," Edith wailed. "What if he goes
away and takes you with him? I'll be all alone again."

Little Bear didn't like this idea at all.

"You stop crying, Edith," he coaxed. "I'll put all the clothes away. I'll even tell Mr. Bear I'm sorry."

Edith and Little Bear worked so hard that everything
was tidy in no time.

They found Mr. Bear reading his paper.

"Well?" he said.

"I'm sorry," Edith said softly. "I don't really think you're a bit silly."

"Yes, we're sorry," admitted Little Bear, "and we cleaned everything up."

"And we won't do it again," declared Edith.

"Well now," said Mr. Bear, "in that case I think perhaps we can forget all about it."

"Oh, thank you, thank you, Mr. Bear," cried Edith, hugging him. "I do just love you. I've been so happy since you came to be my friends. Please, will you promise to stay with me forever?"

"Yes, forever," promised Mr. Bear solemnly.

"Forever and ever!" shouted Little Bear.

And they did!